MR. POTTY MOUTH

Roger Mee-Senseless

Warning: This book contains swearing

but if you didn't already realise that, you're a fucking idiot

Mr Potty Mouth's love affair with swearing began at an early age. If he'd had to ability of speech aged 1 second then he would surely have screamed 'fuuuuuuuuuuuuuuucck' as he was being born as if he was riding a log flume, which if you think about it, he sort of was.

At nursery, when other children were learning how to spell 'dog' and 'cat', Mr Potty Mouth was spelling words like 'bollocks', 'dicksplash' and 'shit for brains'.

Yes, Mr Potty Mouth loved a good swear word, in fact he loved more than one, he loved many.

But his favourite, above all, was the 'F bomb'. It was just so versatile it could literally be used in any occasion.

It had, however, got him into trouble on numerous occasions.

This was his English school report from Year 11...

SCHOOL REPORT
Subject area: English
Grade: F (which is apt)

Rordon is an able pupil but his recent essay showed a distinct lack of variety of vocabulary. The references to Roddy Doyle are fair but after running Rordon's essay through a filter I found it to contain no less than 4,282 swear words.

The essay was 5,000 words long...

Upon leaving school, Mr Potty Mouth embarked on a promising football career, where his swearing ways didn't represent much of a problem. Apart from getting sent off occasionally for calling the referee a barrage of names that would make a sailor blush.

However his football plans were cut short by a serious knee injury and he was consequently released by his club, Glasgow Rangers.

After being released he fell into a number of different jobs. The first one was on the customer services counter at the local supermarket.

Whoever thought he would be a suitable person to talk to the public should seriously question their judgement skills.

It was all fine and rosy for the first 45 minutes but then this happened...

He was such a megalomaniac that wherever he worked, he considered the establishment to be 'his' after less time than it takes to play a football match.

His next job was in a library. This one lasted much longer (1 hour 28 mins). The library was packed with people reading in silence and studying when someone returned a book, late.

"FUCK ME! THIS IS 3 FUCKING WEEKS LATE! ARE YOU ACTUALLY TAKING THE FUCKING PISS?! GET OUT OF MY FUCKING LIBRARY, YOU DISGRACE."

After several other failed jobs he finally hit upon cooking. 'It's ideal,' thought Mr Potty Mouth. 'I can literally GET PAID FOR SWEARING AT PEOPLE!!!'. It's the dream ticket!

I just need to become the head chef as quickly as possible then no one will be safe - the other chefs, the waiting staff, the managers, the customers, my gran, I can tell them all to fuck off whenever I feel like it

This attitude stood him in good stead and before long he was, indeed, running his own kitchen.

Being a head chef kept him very busy. When he was busy he got stressed. And when he got stressed he swore. Even more than usual.

Before long a TV production company realised that people LOVED to watch someone tell someone else to FUCK OFF on TV and Rordon's stock began to rise. I mean figuratively, if a pot of stock had actually boiled over he would've hit the roof.

Mr Chef got used to a jet set lifestyle where big TV companies would pay for him to fly to the other side of the world so that he could tell people who lived there to fuck off.

But all travel had been put on hold because of a pandemic so he had to find work closer to home.

Someone had approached him to judge a cookery competition, which he had readily accepted.

Mr Chef drove to the venue in his fancy sports car.

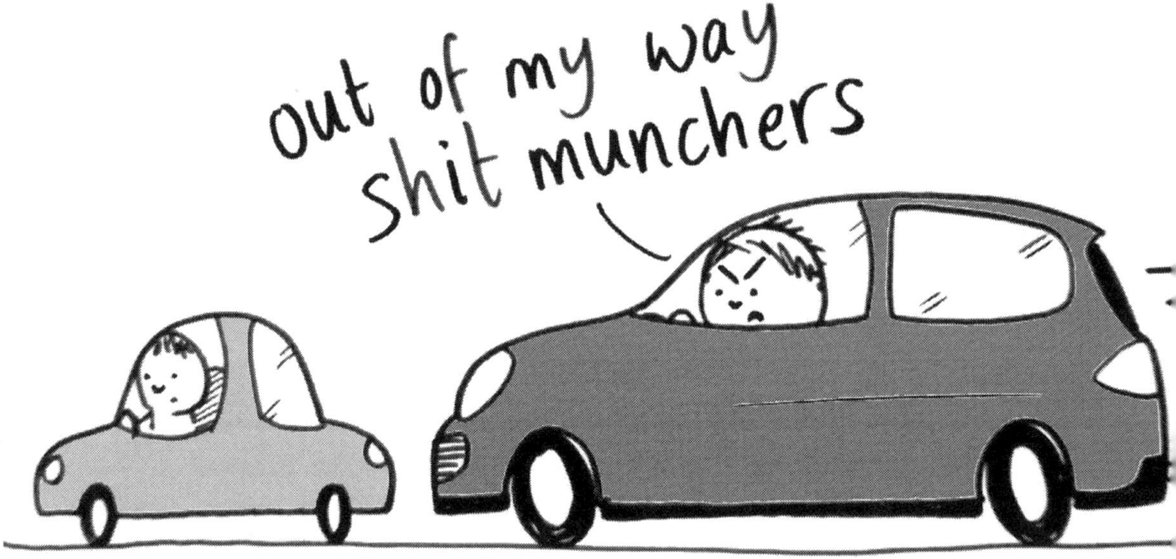
out of my way
shit munchers

"I'm here." said Mr Chef.
"Fuck me, can we get on with this? What are you lot playing at?"

Mr Chef met the contestants and was given the first sample - a plate of cookies.

"Well, they look like cowpats, so not a great start."

He took a bite.

"Jesus Christ, these are drier than the Sahara Desert in a thousand year drought. Someone get me a glass of water, now."

A glass of water was quickly produced.

"Fuck me!" screamed Mr Potty Mouth. "Have you not seasoned this water?" Amateur.

"I think I would've actually preferred to eat a cow pat rather than that cookie. Next.

A few eyebrows were raised but Mr Potty Mouth was passed the next dish. A Ceaser Salad.

"Wow, that salad looks limper than

a 100 year old man's flaccid member. And the chicken looks like it's been eaten and regurgiated. He took a bite. Which he then promptly spat out into the face of the cook responsible.

"Clean that up, you mess!" said Mr Potty Mouth. "Fuck me."

The next dish was a spaghetti carbonara.

Mr Potty Mouth picked up a piece of spaghetti and held it in front of the cook's face.

"Perfectly cooked spaghetti," said Mr Potty Mouth.

The cook beamed with relief.

"Perfectly cooked spaghetti, cooked for the correct amount of time and at the correct temperature, shouldn't snap!"

The cook hung her head in shame and mumbled something about Al dente.

"Al dente? Al dente? Who the fuck is Al dente? Does he know how to cook spaghetti properly?"

"If he does then by all means go and get him because I can't eat this pile of crap."

The last dish presented to Mr Potty Mouth was the dessert course.

"It's an apple pie with butterscotch sauce," said the cook, her voice trembling.

"Well, it looks... okay I suppose." The cooks face brightened a little.

But then he tasted it.

"FUCK ME! How much butter is in this sauce?"

"Erm, erm, I'm sorry I can't remember," came the reply.

"I hope you've got an ambulance on standby, I can literally feel my arteries clogging up as I'm talking, and I'm Scottish!"

"Have you got your own cow on site or have you got a million pounds worth of shares in Clover?"

"Jesus Christ, I can't eat any more of that mess."

"I can't take any more of this. I've got a fucking OBE you know and you serve me up with this shit. It's a disgrace, you're a disgrace. I want a written apology right now."

The contestant began to cry.

"What are you 6 years old or something? GROW UP!" said Mr Chef. "Jesus fucking Christ!"

"I'm 5 actually," came the trembling reply.

It was at this point that Mr Potty Mouth was politely asked to leave Sunnyvale Church of England Primary School. Their cooking competition would have to remain unjudged.

Mr Potty Mouth had to be escorted from the premises in a headlock.

He shouted all kinds of threats and said, "If you touch this hair I will sue you for all you're worth and I'll burn your poxy school to the ground. Just you wait and see!"

When he got home Mr Potty Mouth's wife asked him if he'd had a nice day at work.

Mr Potty Mouth said, "I did as it goes, it was very pleasant indeed. Nothing out of the ordinary.

"What's for tea?" he asked.

"Do you just fancy a greasy kebab?" she said.

"Fuck me," said Mr Potty Mouth.

COOKING FOR MORONS

(THAT'S YOU, IF YOU DIDN'T REALISE — WHICH, IF YOU DIDN'T MAKES YOU EVEN MORE OF A MORON).

CORN FLAKES

Corn Flakes. Classic. Very sweet. Lots of sugar. Wow. They need something to balance the sweetness. Okay. Fuck me.
Salt.
Season liberally.
More.
More.
More.
Not too much, you donkey. Fuck Me. Wow.
Pour on milk from a height.
Beautiful.

Eat.
Don't get it all over your chin, you absolute mess.
Wash up bowl.
Put back in cupboard.
Go back to bed.
Wow.
Done.

CHEESE ON TOAST

Bread. Slice.
Cheese. Slice. Wow. Beautiful.
Give it a sniff. Smells like an old flip flop. Nice.
Place cheese on the bread. Grill. Watch.
Don't watch it burn, you idiot sandwich.
Remove.
Season with salt and pepper.
Plate up. Chair. Sit.
Cutlery. Use. Place in mouth.
Chew. (the food, not the cutlery).
Swallow. Repeat.
Done.

A CUP OF TEA

Take your favourite brand of tea bag. If it's Typhoo then fuck off now. Place in a mug. Nice.
Pour boiling water from a height, the top of the stairs is good. Get your child to hold the cup. Okay. Leave it to brew for 5 minutes exactly, or just mash the bag into the side of the cup for a few seconds. Same difference.
Fuck me. Wow.
Add sugar and milk till it's the colour of Dale Winton or David Dickinson if you like it really strong. Season with salt. Done.

A POT NOODLE

Boil kettle.
Remove sachet and tear open
Pour boiling water to the line
Cover
Wait for 5 mins
Stir in sachet
Grab a spoon
Go outside and use the spoon to dig a hole 6 inches deep
Throw the fucking pot noodle in there and fill it in, you disgusting pig

Reassess your life

TOP TIPS

1. Always remember to season generously.
2. I mean EVERYTHING. Including your drinks. Season water. Season wine.
3. Season your seasonings. Sprinkle table salt over sea salt to add an extra kick.
4. Swear. If things go wrong then swear, it makes you feel better. If things go right then swear to celebrate. Fuck yeh.
5. Did I mention seasoning?

Printed in Great Britain
by Amazon

35231746R00018